The Very MeSsy MeRmAiD

By Tracey Corderoy

Illustrated by Kate Leake

ALISON GREEN BOOKS

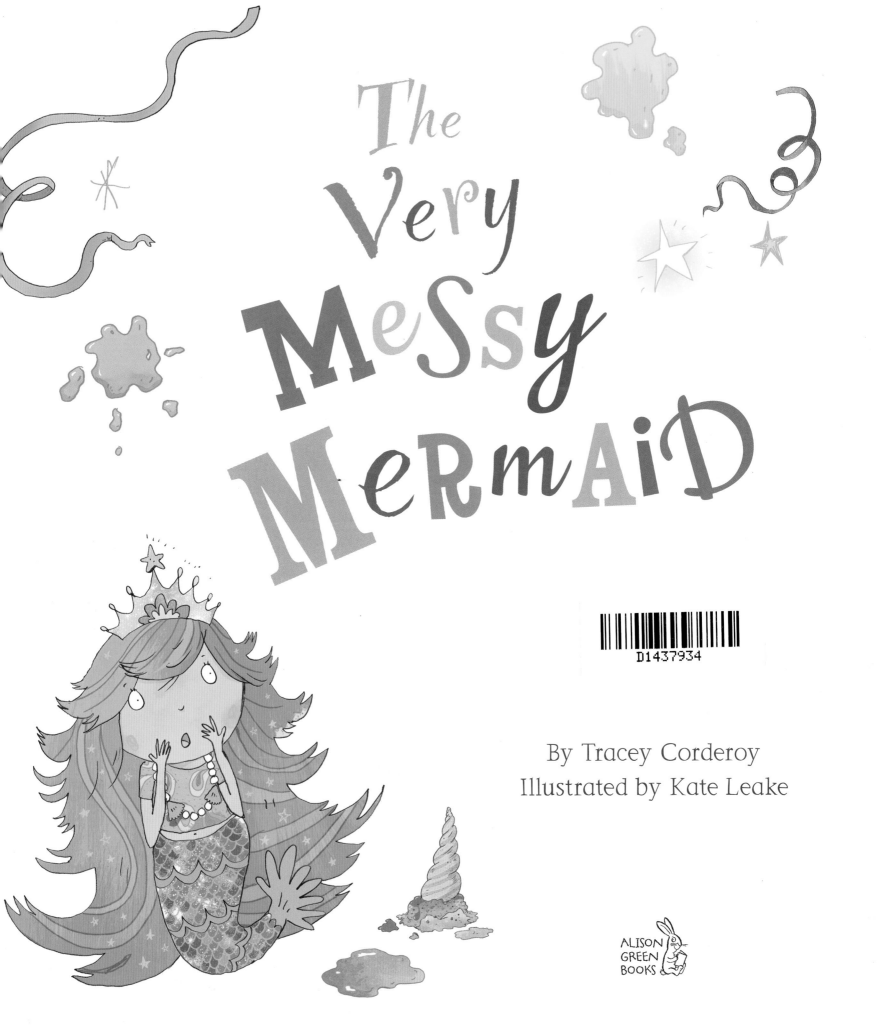

Little Mermaid Twinkletail was the neatest, tidiest mermaid in the ocean. She always hung her clothes up in nice, smart rows. She polished her pet dolphin, Dave, until he shone.

And her super-sparkly
shell collection was . . .

"Perfect!"

Sometimes she wondered how it might feel to get just a *teeny* bit mucky. But she never did, because her mummy and daddy were so proud of their neat little girl. And the ONE thing they hated more than *anything* else was mess!

Ugh!

CASTLE RULES

No cake!

No games!

No friends!

So they never had cake. "In case of crumbs!"
They never played games. "In case things break!"
And they NEVER had friends around to play.
"Because friends make a frightful mess!"

But they did love their little girl very much, so when it was
Twinkletail's birthday, they agreed that she **must** have a party!
(As long as it was very, very neat . . .)

They wrote lots of invitations in their neatest handwriting . . .

Dear Friend,

Although we'd love to invite you to
Twinkletail's very NEAT birthday party,
we're afraid you'd make a dreadful mess
so please don't come!

Lots of love,
Twinkletail's mummy and daddy xxx

SEMPER NITIDUS

"But I thought all parties had friends?" said Twinkletail. "Not this one!" beamed her mummy. "This party is going to be special! (And very, very neat!)"

Twinkletail's very neat party began with a birthday feast – one small, ever-so-tidy **water biscuit!** An octopus stood on guard to sweep up the crumbs.

"Delicious!" cried her daddy.
"Yum, yum!"

Next, they played
Don't-Pass-The-Parcel.
Twinkletail held the parcel very neatly without ripping off any wrapping paper
"Lovely!" beamed her mummy.
"Well done!"

They were just playing **Un-Musical Chairs,**
(which meant not moving at all) when suddenly,
the telephone rang.

It was Twinkletail's Fairy Godmother.
"Happy Birthday, my dear!" she said.
"It's time for your birthday wish!"

Twinkletail knew exactly what she wanted.
"I wish I could have a **normal** party," she whispered,
"with a friend to play with, and proper games – and a cake!
But Mummy and Daddy would never allow it."
"Ahhh," her Fairy Godmother said, "maybe this year, they will!"

And a swirl of magical stars came dancing out of the telephone.

The sparkly stars **whooshed** through the castle, dusting each room with bright sprinkles. They bounced off the freshly cleaned windows and floors. They pinged off the polished vases. And they twirled around Twinkletail's mummy and daddy, showering them in magic!

Just then, there was a knock at the door. A friend had come to the party. "Shall I tell her to go away?" asked Twinkletail. "She might make a mess." **"Who minds mess?"** beamed her parents. **"We don't!"**

Twinkletail gasped. "Really?" she said. What had happened to her mummy and daddy? Her Fairy Godmother must have done some **amazing** magic!

"Let's play a game!" cried Twinkletail's daddy.
"Pass-The-Parcel-Polo-
Pandemonium!"

"Jump on a seahorse!" her mummy shouted,
giving the parcel a whack. "Whoever
makes the most mess is the winner!"

But everyone made so much mess they were all winners!
"What can we play next?" asked Twinkletail, hoping
they wouldn't say Un-Musical Chairs.

But her daddy shouted,
"Let's have a DISCO!"

He started to jig about like a wild thing
as the magical stars swirled around him.
Then everyone piled on to the dance floor . . .

and the ocean ROCKED!

All that dancing made them hungry.
"We could have another water biscuit?"
Twinkletail said.

"A water biscuit? Pah!" her daddy cried.
"We need a proper birthday feast!"
He clapped his hands and in it came . . .

All the messiest food imaginable!

Big sloppy trifles,
super-sticky ice cream
and mountains of wobbly jelly!

Everyone dived in. They ate and ate!

Then, it was time for . . .

... the birthday cake!

They all sang "Happy Birthday".
Then Twinkletail took a big, deep breath
and blew out her candles ...

But as the flickering flames disappeared,
the magical stars vanished, too. Twinkletail's
parents looked around at their messy, sticky castle.
"Whatever's been going on?" they cried.
They couldn't remember a thing.

"I've just had the best party ever!" said Twinkletail.
"But you can't have!" they gasped. "There's so much mess!"
Yet, strangely, their little girl looked really happy.

Twinkletail's daddy thought for a moment.
"Did you make a wish when you blew out your candles?"
Twinkletail shook her head.
"Good!" said her daddy. "May I borrow that wish?"

"All right," said Twinkletail sadly.
Her daddy would wish that their messy castle
was neat and tidy again. Then, all the fun would be over.

Her daddy closed his eyes, and he said,
"I wish that our castle was . . .

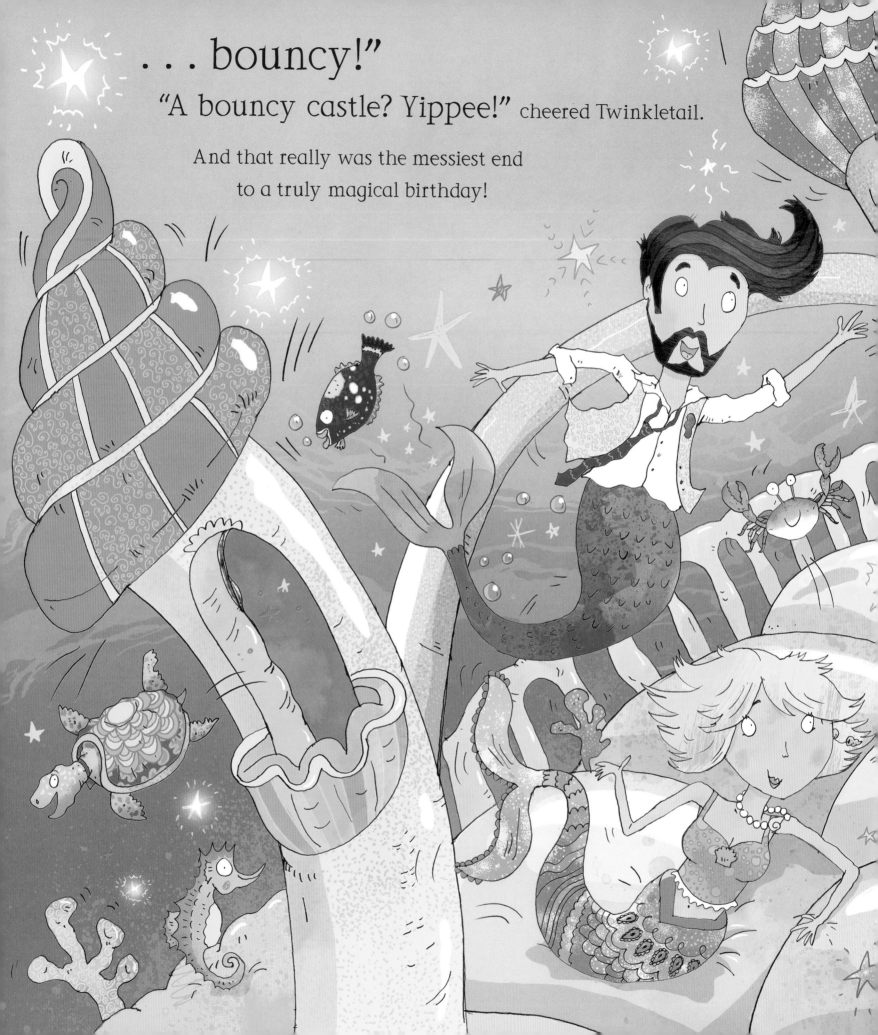

. . . bouncy!"

"A bouncy castle? Yippee!" cheered Twinkletail.

And that really was the messiest end
to a truly magical birthday!

For Anna and Charlotte, with my love xx – T.C.
For my star of a sister, Eleanor – K.L.

First published in 2013 by Alison Green Books
This edition published in 2019
An imprint of Scholastic Children's Books
Euston House, 24 Eversholt Street
London NW1 1DB
A division of Scholastic Ltd
www.scholastic.co.uk
London – New York – Toronto – Sydney – Auckland
Mexico City – New Delhi – Hong Kong
This paperback edition first printed in 2018

Text copyright © 2013 Tracey Corderoy
Illustrations copyright © 2013 Kate Leake

ISBN: 978 1 407193 23 6

Papers used by Scholastic Children's Books are made from
wood grown in sustainable forests.